Mommy Moon

by Jarvel Noble

Mommy Moon
Jarvel Noble

Limits of Liability and Disclaimer of Warranty
The author and publisher shall not be liable for your misuse of this material. This book is strictly for informational purposes. The purpose of this book is to educate and entertain. The author and publisher do not guarantee anyone following these techniques, suggestions, tips, ideas, or strategies will become successful. The author and publisher shall have neither liability nor responsibility to anyone with respect to any loss or damage caused, or alleged to be caused, directly or indirectly by the information contained in this book. Views expressed in this publication do not necessarily reflect the views of the publisher.

Printed in the United States of America
Keen Vision Publishing, LLC
www.publishwithkvp.com
ISBN: 979-8-9927392-0-6

For my loving sons, Bryson, our gift that never stops giving,'and Greyson, the gift we prayed for. May you know that Mom loved you two dearly. May you forever feel her presence. May she forever live in your hearts, and watch over you in this journey called life.

For Thomas, Woodard, Jones, Noble family and all the loved ones we have lost along the way.

Thanks to our growing village who has shown an unwavering outpour of love and encouragement. Thank you for uplifting us over the years. For the numerous phone calls, texts, cards, we are eternally grateful for every single one of you — city to city, state to state. May this book be encouraging after the loss of a loved one. The sun will shine again and may your joy be restored.

♥ *Bryson, Greyson, Jarvel*

One day my family was very sad. "Mommy's body stopped working. Mommy has gone to heaven to rest forever," Daddy told me.

I was confused. Mommy never left without giving me plenty of hugs and kisses. I thought to myself, "Maybe she had to leave in a hurry." I was sure she would give me lots of hugs and kisses after our bedtime story that night.

But bedtime came, and Mommy was not there.

When I woke up, I dashed into Mommy and Daddy's bedroom. "Good morning!" I yelled.

Daddy was still sad and Mommy still was not there. "Mommy is gone to heaven. That is where she will be sleeping from now on," Daddy told me.

I became sad just like Daddy.

"It is okay to cry," Daddy told me, "Mommy is gone forever, and we cannot see her anymore. This is called *death*. Death makes us sad and angry. It makes us want to cry. These emotions are part of a process called *grieving*."

Daddy told me we were going to celebrate her life with something called a *funeral*. At the funeral, I saw all of my family and Mommy's friends. Everyone was crying. There were lots and lots of pretty flowers, and people took turns telling funny stories about Mommy.

At the cemetery, we all said our final goodbyes to Mommy. I missed her so much. I was still very sad.

Everything was different after Mommy left...

On my first day of kindergarten, I was very nervous. It was hard going to school without Mommy. She would walk me inside and give me big hugs to calm the nervous butterflies in my heart.

But Mommy is gone. So now, Daddy takes me to school.

"Daddy," I called to him before we left, "Mommy always calls Grandma before I go to school."

One night, I was riding home with my family and we noticed the moon. It shined bright against the black night sky. It seemed to be following us down the road.

"The moon is beautiful. It looks like your mommy," my aunt pointed out.

I gasped. "It is my mommy! My mommy is following us!" I yelled out.

We pulled over to get a picture with the beautiful moon in the sky.

Mommy and I loved the beach – dolphins, sand castles, and playing in the ocean waves. I was always super excited about the beach every year. We used to sing our favorite songs the whole car ride.

The first time I went to the beach without her, I felt nervous. I played with my cousins at the beach. When they needed water, they ran to their mommies. I had no mommy to run to. I felt alone and sad, but I tried to cheer up and play with my cousins again.

Mommy and I loved the holiday season. But holidays felt different since Mommy was gone.

On Halloween, I wore my favorite costume. On Thanksgiving, I stuffed my belly full. On Christmas, I left cookies and milk for Santa on Christmas. Even though I did all the things I did with Mommy, the holidays still were not the same without her.

"Holidays may never feel the same again, son. I hope the memories you and Mommy made bring you joy when you feel down," Daddy told me.

Even though some days were very hard and felt really long, time went by fast. I got bigger, graduated from kindergarten, lost my first tooth, and learned how to ride my bike without training wheels. I also worked hard to become a good big brother!

I started playing sports and wore Mommy's favorite number, 22, because her birthday was March 22nd. I received a lot of school and sports awards.

Dad said I got my brains and athleticism from Mommy. I always wished she were there to see me growing up. I want to make her proud.

Some days, I suddenly get sad without warning and cry again. But Dad is always right there to cheer me up. It feels good to see my dad smiling and laughing again. He shows me pictures and videos of Mommy and our family. He shows me the places we have gone and the things we have done. I cannot remember it all because I was a baby. But it does put a smile on my face.

As the years go by, it is still hard without Mommy. I have my fun, goofy, and silly days, but some days, I still feel grief.

I always think about her voice, her laugh, her hugs and kisses, and how she made me feel so loved. I feel like a piece of my heart went to heaven the day Mommy left us.

I try hard not to forget all the memories I made with her. As I make new memories, she is in my heart. It feels like she is right there with me.

Mommy,

I miss your bear hugs, juicy kisses, and playtime. I miss your beautiful face and smile that lit up the whole room. I miss your voice calling my name. I miss you…

I cannot physically see you anymore, but I know you are always watching over me. Whenever I miss you, memories always bring me comfort. You are my guardian angel up above. Each night, I see you in the night sky and tell you goodnight.

I'll love you forever. You're always with me, Mommy Moon.

Our Beacon of Love and Light

Courtney Danielle Thomas Noble

Born on March 22, 1988, in Tuscaloosa, Alabama, to Cheryl Thomas Cutsumbis and Rodney Keith Jones, Courtney Danielle Thomas Noble was a beacon of love and light to all who knew her. From an early age, she confessed her love for the Lord at Bethel Baptist Church and later became a devoted member of The Movement Fellowship Church in Pratt City, Alabama.

Courtney's roots were firmly planted in Birmingham, where she excelled both academically and athletically. As the valedictorian of Erwin High School's class of 2006, Courtney's academic prowess was matched only by her talents on the basketball and volleyball courts. Her accolades included being elected Homecoming Queen, a testament to her captivating presence and endearing personality.

Courtney's journey continued as she graduated from the University of Alabama in 2010 with a Bachelor of Science in Accounting while nurturing her lifelong love for Alabama Football and the Crimson Tide. During her time at the university, she met her soulmate, Jarvel, whom she later married, and together they welcomed two beautiful sons, Bryson and Greyson.

Courtney's professional life was marked by her dedication and excellence. As a former participant in the prestigious InRoads leadership program, she went on to serve Vulcan Materials with distinction for over 15 years. Her infectious smile and captivating personality were a testament to her ability to connect with everyone she encountered, never meeting a stranger.

Courtney's zest for life was evident in her love for travel, exploring the world, and creating cherished memories with her beloved family and friends. Tragically, on August 12, 2021, at the tender age of 33, the Lord called Courtney home to eternal rest. Yet, her legacy lives on, not only through the lives of her devoted husband and children but in the countless hearts she touched during her 33 years on this earth.

About the Author

Jarvel Maurice Noble is a passionate writer whose personal experiences have inspired this story. Born in the rural black-belt area of York, Alabama, to Cora Noble and James Marshall, Jarvel's life has been shaped by the joys and challenges of family.

After the untimely passing of his wife, Courtney, Jarvel found solace in the written word, channeling his grief and love into the creation of "Mommy Moon." As a widowed father of two sons, Bryson and Greyson, Jarvel draws from his profound understanding of the impact a parent's loss can have on a child, infusing his work with authenticity and empathy.

Jarvel holds a Bachelor of Science in Business Administration from the University of Alabama and a Master of Science in Sports Management from the United States Sports Academy. A retired Army veteran, Jarvel currently resides in Birmingham, Alabama, where he enjoys spending time with his family, traveling, and exploring his passions for music, sports, art, and reading.

www.ingramcontent.com/pod-product-compliance
Lightning Source LLC
Chambersburg PA
CBHW041005170626
46815CB00002B/166